WINTER

STORIES, ARTICLES, & PHOTOGRAPHS

BY SANDRA GRACE

Sandra Fram

AUTHOR, EDITOR, & DESIGNER
SANDRA GRACE

WEBSITE
WINGSINTHESTORM.CA

STOCK PHOTOS
SON OF GOD, SON OF MAN; THE VISIT;
FIRST PROMISE; NEVERGREEN TREE

ADVENTURE NORTH PHOTOS
GRACE FRAM

THE WALL PHOTOS
SANDRA GRACE & FROM MY FATHER'S PHOTO ALBUM

ALL OTHER PHOTOS
SANDRA GRACE

FICTION
FIRST PROMISE; THE VISIT; NEVERGREEN TREE

COPYRIGHT © 2024 BY SANDRA GRACE

FIRST EDITION

Published by SANDRA FRAM

WINTER

Lace

by Sandra Grace

How special are those intermissions from life that come out of nowhere...those intervals that are infused with a beauty you didn't expect...the ones that make you forget your worries for just a moment so you can soak in their magnificence.

It was the 29th of April, back in 2013. I was on my way to my tiny attic apartment on Ominica Street in Moose Jaw after another long shift at work. I was eager to get home, weary with the familiar aches and stiffness that came from scrubbing showers.

I stood alone on the sidewalk at the corner of Fairford and Main, waiting for the walk light. The darkness of approaching midnight wrapped around me like an Angora shawl. At that hour, the streets were empty, and it was as if the whole city belonged to me.

On the opposite corner stood City Hall with its clock tower. The building reminded me of the old post office on Main Street in Moncton, my hometown. As always, I gazed, captivated by its marvelous stone blocks, smooth pillars, and regal dome.

As the hands of the clock ticked away the last few minutes of the day, huge snowflakes drifted slowly, silently to the ground. There before me, the streets transformed into an enchanting fantasy as nature draped its finest lace over the downtown. The intricately woven covering, fresh and white, sparkled in the light like tiny diamonds scattered across the ground.

I forgot how tired I was; I forgot my hurry to get home. Slowly, I turned to take in the scene from every direction—Winter's encore, interrupting the Saskatchewan Spring. Smile growing ever bigger, I breathed in the cool, pure air and reveled in the quiet stillness and splendor of the night.

The beautiful, ordinary *everyday*...often the source of your most tranquil moments and uplifting memories...the small respites amidst your cares.

Adventure North

BY SANDRA GRACE
PHOTOGRAPHS BY GRACE FRAM

"We flew over the wintery terrain, feeling the spray of snow and the sting of the wind on our faces."

For days, we kept eager eyes on the weather, hoping with everything in us that the arctic blast would let up in time.

I'd come to Grande Prairie, Alberta earlier that week to find it shrouded in ice fog. Temps had dipped to -42, colder if you counted the wind chill. Old Man Winter was testing the -50-degree mark, taking a bite out of anyone who dared step out into his domain.

But my daughter had planned a Christmas Eve adventure for us—herself, her five-year-old son, and me—and come December 24th, anything below -25 degrees Celsius would mean our event would have to be cancelled, and we'd be out of luck.

Then came the reprieve. By mid-afternoon on Christmas Eve, the temperature hit a balmy -23! Excitedly, we pulled on layers of pants, sweaters, socks, and mittens—bound up in fleece and wool, like we'd raided a sheep farm—and we set off for our excursion.

We pulled into the parking lot and left the warm vehicle behind. It was just a short walk through the trees to the staging area. Stepping into the clearing, I felt like a kid, unable to suppress my wide-eyed glee. The tingling inside me grew, filling and warming me, even while I shivered in the cold. I'd never imagined I'd get to do something like this...

Around the perimeter were a dozen snow-covered, A-frame houses—unusual little structures on stilts. The residents padded over and greeted us, their wet noses nudging at our mittens. They were gorgeous creatures, sleek and strong, with thick coats of black, grey, tan, and white. And today, these beautiful dogs would give us the ride of a lifetime, pulling the sled that would transport us into an encounter unlike anything we'd ever known.

The dogs were quickly tethered, pair by pair, to the gangline that latched to the sled. They were itching for the run. Their tails wagged, and they pranced in place, betraying their impatience with us humans who took too long to get on board.

Our sled, outfitted with blankets and canvas wrapping, was at the ready, and I eased my bulky self down into its cocoon. My grandson sat on my lap, and we were tucked in and tightly fastened up to our necks. The remaining two riders stood: my daughter at the front handlebar, directly behind us, and our musher at the back handlebar, behind her.

And with a chorus of *woofs* and *yips*, we were off, skimming across a track of white that cut through the woodland. Like the lilt of a song came the swish of the runners on the snow. We flew over the wintery terrain, feeling the spray of the snow and the sting of the wind on our faces. The dogs, in their boundless energy, were doing what they were born to do. I swear they were laughing.

Eventually, the trail widened, and we pulled to a stop. In minutes, our musher had a fire burning, and we were sipping hot chocolate and warming our toes. Stately trees stood guard over us while we rested, savoring each minute—the crisp air, every sight and sound, each breath of the forest. What if we could stay right here...if we could ride these trails forever...?

The shuffling of paws on the ground hinted that our delay should be brief. The dogs called out their eagerness for us to be on our way. We loaded up and were back on the run.

Light grey skies hung over us as we sped through the woods, and snow-laden branches seemed to reach for us as we passed. Big white flakes filled the air, and the whole world quieted, even the runners on the snow, like the whisper of fairy wings. Everything around us was draped in a haze—an alabaster veil—obscuring its lines, fading the image, as if a sweet moment suddenly recalled from a dream...

It was just a glimpse for us into another world—what was once a way of life for the people of the north. One quick step into an enchanted land, enveloped in the magic of winter, on a journey we wished would never end.

Sandra Grace Photography

STOCK PHOTO

SON OF GOD SON OF MAN

The baby's cries break the stillness of the night. His little fists flail as his mother unwraps him and changes the soiled strips of cloth for fresh swaddling bands. She pulls him closer and coos softly to quiet him. The rustling of hay in the stalls...the lowing of cattle...the pounding of hooves in the dirt are the music of a lullaby. She strokes his velvet cheek. She smiles into his pinched, round face and marvels at his newborn perfection. "Beautiful boy," she whispers.

Her baby is much like any other baby born into the world. He cries when he's hungry; he shivers when he's cold; he soothes at the sound of her voice and snuggles into her embrace. In time, he'll learn to crawl. He'll pull himself awkwardly to his feet and take his first steps. He'll stumble and fall; she'll wipe his tears and clean his scrapes. He'll curl up on her lap as she teaches him the Scriptures. He'll study math and practice shaping his letters. He'll learn and grow like every other child.

But this baby's not like any other. Her baby is the Holy Son of Yahweh. This little one, born into poverty, is King, master and owner of the universe. These cries are the voice that spoke the world into existence. This helpless infant is the God who formed man out of the dust and breathed life into his lungs.

He is Emmanuel (God with us), stepped down from the splendor of Heaven into this world of evil and sorrow. He's taken on the form of the fallen ones, His created. One of us, living among us.

Sinless One, subjecting Himself to imperfect parents. Omniscient One, under instruction by fallible minds. The Omnipotent, restricted by hunger, fatigue, pains, mental and physical ends. He is deity wrapped in flesh; spirit confined to a body; the eternal set in time; holiness amidst depravity; limitless bound by the laws of physics.

Still, He is El Shaddai (all Sufficient One), Adonai (the Lord), El Elyon (the God Most High), and the Great I Am.

He is the innocent one, the Lamb, the perfect sacrifice, born to die...to suffer the wrath of God that sinful man deserves.

He is Savior. Redeemer.

All this, He chooses for a purpose decreed in eternity past: salvation, freely offered to all; forgiveness, granted to those who repent.

But death will not be the end, for He is Yeshua, the risen Lord. The Life. Victor over the tomb and conqueror of the grave. He will take His place at the right hand of His Father in Heaven, alive evermore. El Olam (Everlasting God).

Jesus, the Lion of Judah; the Judge, fierce and righteous. Praise and honor, glory and majesty be to Him forever, King of kings, Savior God.

This little baby, the promised Messiah...

...Child like no other, her beautiful boy.

And the Word became flesh and dwelt among us.
John 1:14.

THE VISIT

by Sandra Grace

They descended upon her with a flurry of luggage and crying babies. The front door stood ajar as they carried in bag after bag, letting the late-January wind brisk through the tiny apartment, chilling her to the bone. She stepped forward twice to close the door; but each time, they threw it open again, slamming the wall, and still departed without shutting it behind them.

The mound on the living room floor grew till it overflowed down the narrow hallway and spilled into the kitchen. She stepped gingerly over their piles of toys and winter gear, thinking her Texas family may have overdone it with the down-filled coats and ski pants, toques and woolen socks. She took hold of a suitcase and started for the guest bedroom, then realized she didn't know which belonged to whom so put it down again. She stood, hands clasped in front of her, not knowing what to do. She hated feeling useless with so much activity bustling around her.

When at last their cars were emptied, they caught her up in warm hugs and glowing smiles: her daughter, Katherine, and son-in-law, John; their son, Ryan, and Ryan's wife, Kayla; and Ryan and Kayla's three children. "It's so good to finally meet you, Nana," Kayla beamed.

"I'm so happy you all could come," she smiled.

"Kids, say hello to Great Nana," Kayla called.

Five-year-old McKinley peeked out from behind her mother, apparently struck mute upon seeing Great Nana's crinkled face and snow white hair. "I'm pleased to meet you, McKinley," she extended her hand. But the little girl only cowered deeper into the safety of her mother.

Baby Hayden yawned from his father's football hold and snuggled back into sleep. And 19-month-old Maverick was already standing on the arm of the loveseat, pulling a snow globe down from the buffet. Whatever happened to ordinary names like Susan, Michael, and Stephen?

"I'll show you to your rooms." She led Ryan and Kayla to the guestroom where Christmas candles still shone brightly from the windowsill. She'd done up the bed with her best handmade quilt and matching pillow covers, and she'd placed her favorite lamp on the bedside stand, all because she'd wanted them to feel welcome.

"The kids can go in the den." She pointed to the front room—a nook, really. "I borrowed a crib for the baby, and the two older ones can share the pull-out. It's a bit cramped, but it's just for sleeping."

"Oh, no, Nana. The baby sleeps in our room," said Kayla. "I need to be sure he's okay through the night." On cue, Ryan handed Hayden to his wife and began rolling the crib into the other room.

"Suit yourselves," she told them, though she couldn't understand parents these days. Her children had slept in the nursery. Parents, back then, hadn't needed their sleep disturbed by every tiny sigh and rustle of blankets. Well, each to his own...

She continued with her instructions: "Katherine, you and John will have my room..."

"Mom, we're not taking your bed," her daughter insisted.

"You're not taking it. I'm offering. Now, I'll have no argument," she cut off impending protests. "I'll be quite comfortable on the couch." She didn't miss the eye-roll Katherine flashed at John.

The afternoon erupted in nothing less than chaos. The kids had slept on the drive, so there was no naptime relief for the adults now. Maverick scurried from one thing to another, climbing on furniture and grabbing at everything within reach. Katherine stayed on his heels, preventing utter destruction of the apartment while Kayla tried desperately to soothe the screaming infant in the other room.

She slipped into her coat and boots and eased open the door. She'd no more than gotten the shovel in hand and breathed in the quiet of freshly falling snow when John was at her side. "Ma, you shouldn't be doing that." He took the shovel from her and shooed her aside. Did he think her completely incapable? Ryan joined him with the snow scoop and the two went at the walk and the driveway, already forgetting she was there.

Reluctantly, she turned away. They didn't understand. She shoveled for the same reason she persisted with everything else: because if she stopped, she might not be able to start again.

Back inside, the apartment had gone quiet. The baby was asleep, and Kayla had returned to take charge of Maverick. She watched her granddaughter-in-law...how sweetly she talked to the little ones...how gently she corrected them. And she couldn't help but be impressed. This young mother was attentive and

loving, yet she didn't put up with misbehavior. These children were loved and cared for well.

Her disquieted heart began to settle.

"Nana, can I help you fix dinner?" Kayla asked, and the two of them were soon laughing and chatting, pots clanging in the kitchen, while Katherine kept the children out of trouble.

An hour later, she pulled the turkey from the oven and called her guests. The horde charged in like ravenous wolves, scraping chairs on the hardwood floor and digging into the food before she'd finished getting it all to the table. She quietly took her seat and bowed her head, hoping there'd be something left when she opened her eyes again.

"Would you say grace for all of us, Nana?" Kayla interrupted.

She looked up to see six beautiful faces beaming back at her, expectantly, their plates loaded, yes, but their cutlery still untouched. Her plate, too, had been served.

"Yes, of course." And they bowed together to give thanks for their belated Christmas dinner and for this treasured time with cherished family.

All too soon, their week was over, and they were performing the arrival procedure in reverse—one bag after another reloaded into the cars. This time, she didn't care about the open door. This time, she donned her coat and gloves and helped them with their things.

When the last piece had been stuffed in, they gathered around her, feet shuffling in the cold. "I don't know how you do it, Mom. You keep it all together so nicely. I'm not half as on the ball as you are." Katherine hugged her mother's tiny form, lingering in her warm embrace.

The others scooped her up, one by one, nearly squeezing the breath out of her. The baby cooed from his fleece and fur, and Maverick clung to her legs, giggling. McKinley flew into her arms. "We'll come back tomorrow, Great Nana."

"Well, not tomorrow," chuckled Ryan. "But soon. We promise." He planted a kiss on her cheek.

She watched them head for the cars. She took half a step toward the building but stopped, reluctant to pull away. Her hand came up partway as though pleading with them not to go. Then she let it fall to her side. With the slam of car doors, her head drooped forward just a little, the light catching a glint in her eyes. She watched the vehicles pull out of the parking lot, faces pressed to the windows. "It's going to be awfully quiet here now," she whispered.

Not till they were out of sight did she go back in, out of the cold. The apartment sighed with the hollow sound of the closing door.

...So awfully quiet, now...

STOCK PHOTO

Little Maritimer on the Prairie

I'm *her*...the shivering mound of wool and fleece with the telescope hood and the sleeves drooped over her fingertips—that one who's always cold.

So winter doesn't click with me. By sometime in November I resign myself to the months ahead, I withdraw from activities, and like a turtle pulling into its shell, I tuck into my house and lock the doors. I'd stay till May if I could.

Whether because of some cosmic joke or the stork misread the delivery address is arguable, but somehow I ended up the child of New Brunswick parents. Yes, New Brunswick with its waist-deep snow and ice-laden trees, where the damp cold cuts to the bone, and where June still hoards its stash of the white stuff in the woods and along the tree lines.

As a kid, I couldn't understand why adults disliked winter. What could be better than pond skating and sledding? Maritime snow is wet and heavy—snowmen, snow forts, and snowball fights. Those frigid flakes were once piled so deep in the schoolyard, the older kids made a monstrous tunnel. They let everyone take turns shimmying through. It felt pretty cool for us littles to be included in big-kid activities. Winter's magic has a way of bringing folks together.

Ol' Jack Frost always sent a few blasts harsh enough to cancel school. Blustery mornings, we were all ears, tuned to the radio, anticipating the announcement. Once, even the snowplow couldn't get through for days. Finally, it chiselled a path, leaving 10-foot walls of white on either side of the road. Impressive.

March brought pussy willows and sugar-making; cold nights; warm days; wet socks and mittens. Deep in the woods was a grove of maple trees that my father would tap. My sister and I would play at a brook nearby while he collected the sap (clear; watery; slightly sweet; almost tasteless). Dad would dump the sap into buckets and pull it home on a toboggan. Mom would boil it for hours on the kitchen stove until it got thick and golden brown—40 gallons of sap to make 1 gallon of maple syrup. And you're not a true Maritimer until you've had maple candy on the snow—a taffy delight that gums up the teeth till you can't open your mouth.

Sweet though be these memories, my enthusiasm mysteriously waned after I grew up, and suddenly, anything below 20° C would give me the shivers.

So when I escaped the ferocious Maritimes, where did I go? The Okanagan? Caribbean?

Nope! The Saskatchewan prairies! Where the snow is less, but the cold is more, and the winters seem unending.

Yet, one love from my childhood still remains—that of a good winter storm. There's something soothing about being at home, safe and warm, during a blizzard.

So when the cold prairie winds blow and the snow hits with fury, I'll tuck away in my house to watch Ol' Jack rage past the windows. I'll cozy up to a blazing wood stove, nostalgia wrapped around me like a blanket, warming the body and the soul.

Little Maritimer on the Prairie.

by Sandra Grace

The Wall

by Sandra Grace

I'm standing at the wall, seeing the name etched there, touching the indentations for the first time. Everything else seems to blur and voices fade to a hum. All the facts I've read and the stories I've heard collide in my head till I can't sort one from the other.

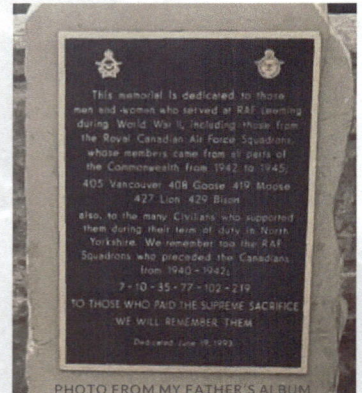

PHOTO FROM MY FATHER'S ALBUM

Not an hour ago, my sister and I pulled into the parking lot here—Nanton, Alberta's Bomber Command Museum of Canada. "Open Saturdays & Sundays," the sign out front proclaimed. Since today is Monday, we won't be touring the museum, but our real interest—the Memorial Wall—is still easily accessible outside.

Sandra Grace Photography

We quickly found what we were looking for. We paused in silence, and we snapped our treasured photographs. We slowly circled the wall and the grounds; reading epitaphs; feeling the gravity of this place.

As we headed back to our car, a door at the rear of the building opened, and a tour group began to spill out into the parking lot. *Maybe the sign out front is wrong,* I thought. So I went over to the guide, who now stood chatting with his guests, and asked, "Is the museum open today?"

"No," he replied with a firm shake of his head, "This group was a special booking." He asked where we were from, and I explained.

Then I added, "Our uncle's name is on the wall over there."

The guide looked at me with knowing eyes and said, "Come inside."

He showed us to a podium that held a big, blue book, *They Shall Grow Not Old.* "You can find your uncle's name in here," he told us.

And we did—a synopsis of Flying Officer Thomas Roland Mellish, his crew, and his fatal flight. More clicking of our cameras.

Our guide seemed unhurried. He made his way around the room, pointing out photographs, one after another, and telling us the stories behind them. He took us out to the hangar to see the Lancaster bomber housed there, explaining that it's the same size as the Halifax bomber our uncle flew. He talked solemnly about remembrance and respect for the men and women who served. His love for this place and for the history it holds could be heard in his every word.

We're outside again now, back at the wall, and our guide is with us. He's inviting us to come again in summer when they will take the Lancaster out to the yard and fire it up for visitors.

But I'm looking at the wall. I reach out to the granite slab. There are 10,673 names engraved here—Bomber Command Canadians who were killed in service. Each name represents a life and purpose, a family left behind, and a future the bearer would never get to see.

And I wonder, have we become complacent in our privileges, those of us who've never seen or heard or felt or tasted war? Do we take for granted their sacrifices and throw away the very things they fought for?

Our freedom comes at a price, paid by the blood of these and many other men and women. Remember them, yes. But preserving this freedom is more than just paying tribute to the fallen. It's boldly speaking out for truth and right. It's protecting our people from any who would harm. It's guarding our country against all that would enslave, without and within.

This is the torch they threw to us as they fell.

May we ever hold it high.

Sandra Grace Photography

STOCK PHOTO

FIRST PROMISE

She lifted her face to the sun, shielding her eyes from the light. A hint of dampness hung in the fresh morning air, still fragrant with dew. She reached her hand upward, considering the lush fruit. "Ah… That one," she whispered to no one, plucking the biggest piece and admiring its perfection. A smile played at the corners of her mouth as she bit into the pear, juicy and sweet.

She continued her walk, wandering among the trees along the river. An eagle flew overhead; she could hear its wings cut the air as it passed. Grasses reached toward the sky. Brilliant colors of wildflowers filled the fields.

The world was still a beautiful place. A different kind of beautiful. Not like before. A tinge of sadness touched her heart. Very beautiful, yes. But not like before.

Footsteps pounded on the path ahead. Someone was coming. She darted off the trail into the thick growth and crouched low. Adam had warned her not to go so far.

She peered through the leaves till she saw a young man round the turn. She held her breath. Had he seen her? Her heart beat faster.

But the young man passed by quickly, without even a glance in her direction. Still, she stayed hidden, not daring to move until he was long out of sight.

An image flashed before her: another time she'd crouched in the bushes to hide …

"Where are you?" the voice called.

She hunched lower, but Adam stood and answered. "I heard you coming, and I was afraid."

It was their first fear. Their first shame.

She saw her husband's terrified eyes, the creases in his brow, his pathetic stance—head lowered and shoulders slumped. Pitiful.

Then it hit her—did she look that way too?

Inside her was a feeling she'd never known before, like something was in there—something evil, roiling and churning; laughing; taunting; loving her for yielding; hating her.

"The woman you gave me," Adam was saying. "She did it. She took the fruit and gave it to me. That's why I ate it."

"What have you done?" God asked her now.

She stood slowly, not daring to look at Him. "It wasn't my fault. The serpent tricked me." She hated the lie. But the truth was so despicable... unspeakable—she'd chosen to disobey.

The voice of God sounded above the battle within her. He cursed the ground because of Adam's sin. The soil would not be as fertile as before and Adam would have to work hard his whole life to get it to produce enough for their survival.

God cursed her because of her sin. She would have many pregnancies, and the births would be excruciating for her. Her family, while bringing her much joy, would now bring much sorrow, too.

But it was what He said to the serpent that affected her most. " ... You will bruise Him, but He will crush you." The first promise of a Savior.

Their Creator looked on her and Adam with compassion. They were completely depraved. Completely guilty. Completely condemned. Completely helpless. Their very lives—their eternal souls—hung in the balance, utterly dependent on His mercy. It wasn't till later that she came to understand this better.

Then the Lord God killed a spotless lamb and made clothes for them to cover their shame. But these coverings couldn't take away their sin. This lamb couldn't purify their blackened hearts. The Creator would one day send another Lamb, the perfect sacrifice. Someone who would take on their sin and clothe them in His righteousness, instead. Someone who would cleanse their hearts and restore them to their God. This was His promise.

Adam believed the promise. She believed it too. Because of their faith, they were redeemed.

STOCK PHOTO

STOCK PHOTO

Everything had changed that day. Driven from their paradise, they would never again see their garden home. They had to make their way in a fallen world. Strife and sorrow followed them; pain and heartache. They tried to honor God; they taught their children of the Creator and of redemption; they taught their children's children. But they were sinful parents, and their children were sinful. The generations became more and more corrupt—hating God; forsaking His truth—until evil enslaved most of humanity. The population increased, and society advanced and flourished; but so did wickedness. It grieved her heart. How much more must it grieve the heart of God?

Eve left her place in the undergrowth and started for home. She still saw the blood of that innocent lamb, poured out for her. Even after all these years, the Creator's promise was still her hope. She knew a Savior would come, born of her seed. For a long time, she'd thought it would be her—that she would be the mother of God's chosen One. By now, she knew that wasn't to be.

———————

Eve would never see that perfect substitute. It would be centuries before the promise would be fulfilled in One called Jesus. He would be born in a stable in Bethlehem, a sweet baby whose purpose on earth would be to die on a cross. It was the Creator's plan from before the beginning:

Jesus, Emmanuel—God from eternity past. He was there at creation, forming man from the dust; there in the garden, pronouncing the curse. Yet He would take on flesh and blood...become a man, Himself. He would walk the earth with the fallen race, still God, still righteous and holy, the Messiah.

He would live a life without sin. His holiness would make him the only worthy substitute. His blood would provide atonement for Eve and for all her descendants who believed and repented of their sin, as she did. He would bring forgiveness to those who trusted in Him. Redemption... Restoration to the Father.

He is the spotless Lamb. The perfect sacrifice. The Promised One.

The hope of Eve and all mankind.

by Sandra Grace

The Book of Genesis doesn't say it was a lamb that God killed, just that He made garments of skins for the man and the woman.

The beginning of 'First Promise'—the story of Eve later in life—is fiction. The retelling of her disobedience and the curse follows the account in Genesis 3; however, Eve's thoughts and feelings here are speculation and are not recorded in the Bible.

Read the true account of Eve and the first promise of a Savior in Genesis 2 & 3; the Savior's sacrifice for us in Isaiah 53; His birth in Luke 2.

Sandra Grace Photography

Nevergreen Tree

It was a drizzly Saturday in mid-November when her husband breezed into the kitchen, swept her up in a hug, and announced, "Guess what! I found us a Christmas tree! Brought it home today."

"Already?" she asked, unable to mask her surprise. Seemed to her a little early to cut a tree.

"Don't worry. It'll be fine," he assured her.

The fact that her normally capable husband had completed this one dreaded annual task without a word of urging from her and with time to spare was somewhat of a gift in itself. She decided not to push the issue.

So that was the end of it... Until a month later.

"Hon, where is our Christmas tree?" she asked one morning. "I'd like to set it up today."

"You haven't even come out to see it," he skirted the question.

She paused from her sewing. "I haven't, no... But, where is it? It's in your shop, right?"

"Uhh... well, not exactly."

She crossed her arms and looked him squarely in the eye. "Where, then?"

"It's, ah...outside."

"I knew it. It's that heap out there in the mud, isn't it?" His sheepish expression was all the answer she needed. "You just left it lying in the dirt all this time?"

He was getting irritated with all her questions. "Don't complain to me about the tree when you're not even interested enough to come look at it." He stalked off.

She didn't see what visitation of the tree had to do with anything.

Minutes later, she heard the door being thrown open, followed by the clomp of her husband's work boots down the hall and into the living room. He plopped the mud-encrusted tree ceremoniously into its stand. "It's a fine tree," he announced.

"It's dead." Anyone could see.

"It's not dead! Look!" And he waved his hands at the upper branches that still boasted a hint of green.

"The whole bottom is brown!" she argued. Indeed, a third of the tree.

"No one will notice once the ornaments are on," he insisted.

"But the needles are falling off. It sounds like it's raining in here!"

"It just needs watering. It will be fine." And he actually believed it.

"It's tilted," she pointed out. "It's going to fall."

"It won't fall! I guarantee it! This tree will never fall!"

So she bit her tongue and vowed to say no more.

She spent the next afternoon going through the motions of decorating the pitiful tree. Several times she paused to gaze at the thing and shake her head. Usually, she at least felt sorry for her bedraggled Christmas tree. Not for this one, though. Nope. Not a bit.

She went back to her work. The mini lights just wouldn't sit right. She heaved a sigh as she reached out to tuck them into the obnoxious branches...

Just one touch—that's all it took. Slowly, her Charlie Brown tree started to lean and... Uh-oh! Oh, no! TIMM-BERRR!

She lunged; she grabbed; she braced. But there was no stopping what comes naturally to dead things. Needles showered down, rivers flowed from the freshly filled tree stand, and with a CRACK, that "just fine" Christmas tree split in two, right down the middle, rotten to the core!

She called her husband at work. "Hon, ya know that tree—that fine tree—the one you guaranteed would never fall?"

"Yes..."

"It fell!"

"I'll fix it when I get home," he sighed.

Enough was enough. "Darling, if you can't bring us a respectable tree, I'm going to get our Christmas tree from now on."

"Good idea!" he declared.

"Starting this year."

"We have a tree this year. It's a fine tree."

"It's not fine. It's dead! The tree is dead!"

"All right, then. *You* go search through the woods to find a Christmas tree." That'll teach her sounded through the phone.

"I will." She hung up the call.

* * *

There were so many gorgeous trees in Jack's Christmas lot. "This one!" the kids called. "No, this one!" Finally, they chose one they all agreed on. "How much? she asked, though she really didn't care.

"Ten dollars," Jack replied with a smile as he stepped forward with his saw.

Ten dollars? She watched her husband hand over the crisp bill.

Ten dollars!! All the Christmas tree wannabes that had been carted in and out of their living room over the years when for ten dollars they could have had this: a dense, shapely tree, fully branched and fully needled!

Ten dollars.

* * *

The new tree—the lush, green tree—stood straight and tall, twinkling brightly in their living room. She smiled and sighed...satisfied.

Her husband winked at her and nodded from the doorway. Even he had to admit that, yes, this was, indeed, the most beautiful Christmas tree they'd ever had.

But he couldn't keep from muttering one last—

"The other tree was fine."

STOCK PHOTO

Sandra Grace Photography

YOU CAN'T GO HOME AGAIN

Our dark Silverado hummed along the country road between stands of bare-limbed trees. Brown fields, still showing patches of green, belied the late December date. "I want to go see the house," my sister had said, and we'd all piled into the truck.

From the back seat, I watched familiar scenes rush past the windows — houses, hills, and farmyards I'd known my whole life. The twists and turns in the road soothed like a lullaby, one I'd heard ten thousand times before

We rounded the bend and came to a stop at the side of the road. "It's still here," my sister said, tugging me back from my thoughts. I looked up to see the old rusted mailbox, leaning slightly, still bearing the name — R. G. Mellish.

And across the road stood the farmhouse with the same gray vinyl siding. The lilac bush still graced the front lawn, and the same twisted apple trees guarded the north side of the yard. I can see us as kids, climbing those trees and gathering lilacs in the spring. I can see us playing in the hayloft of the tin barn and riding over the green ridges beyond.

But a lot of things are not the same here. The familiar is riddled with empty holes. The barn we played in is gone. So is our beloved elm tree that grew next to the road, right in the middle of the driveway.

The people of the house are gone now, too. Our father passed away nine years ago. Our mother lives in town, far from her garden and her rose bushes. My sister and I moved away, as well — she moved first; then, a decade ago, I went too. Somebody else owns the house we grew up in, and their children now play in its fields and climb its trees.

"Let's walk down to the brook," my sister suggested. Our old swimming hole was just a hop and a skip down the road. And there, right at the entrance to the field we had to traverse, was a 'No Trespassing' sign. Neighborhood kids aren't allowed to swim there anymore.

We skirted the field so as not to offend. The brook, we discovered, was overgrown with trees and alder bushes brimming right to its edges, whereas the banks we knew in childhood were wide open and welcoming.

But the same thick-steeled, corrugated culvert — it had to be 20 feet to its top — emptied its frigid water into the same pool we once knew so well. The same boulders, though rearranged, still formed the sides of the pool. This was where hot summer afternoons would find us. In the shallow overflow beyond, I could picture our faithful old dog, tail wagging, darting after minnows for hours.

For all the changes here, the sight of that monstrous, gaping culvert flooded the senses with nostalgia; the gurgling brook with its swirling waters penetrated and soothed the soul.

No, you can't go home again, for home has stretched and purged and grown into something new, and so have you.

But you can revisit it anytime by throwing open your chest of treasured memories, pulling them out, touching their smooth edges, hearing their whispers, breathing in their aromas.

They wait there, forever untarnished, becoming only sweeter and more fragrant with the years.

—————— by Sandra Grace ——————

By Iris Fiorita — Beit She'an, Israel

SANDRA GRACE

Sandra Grace was born and raised in Moncton, New Brunswick. In 2012, she relocated to the prairies of Saskatchewan and Alberta.

Sandra's passion for writing began at the age of eight, inspired by the encouragement of her third-grade teacher.

She discovered her love of photography around her pond in Airdrie, AB and through her exploration of Alberta and Saskatchewan.

In 2020, Sandra spent two months in Costa Rica working on her memoir, *Wings in the Storm: Hope & Healing through Brokenness*, published in 2021.
She is the author of four children's books, under the name, Sandra Fram.

Sandra lives in Shaunavon, Saskatchewan. She works as an administrator; writes for the local paper; and enjoys motorbiking, hiking, photography, travel, family & friends, and of course, writing.

.

BOOKS

Wings in the Storm; Hope & Healing through Brokenness
Prairie
Blossoms
Winter

CHILDREN'S BOOKS

The Secrets of Amethyst Cove

Runaway Teeth

Happy Birthday, Mrs. Gimbal

Priscilla's Leaves
   co-authored with her daughter, Grace

CONTACT HER

sgracewrites@outlook.com
facebook.com/sandra.grace.10048379

WEBSITE

wingsinthestorm.ca

"First Promise,"
"The Visit," &
"Nevergreen Tree"
are fiction.

All other stories and articles in *Winter* are taken from real events.